J is for Jack-O'-Lantern

A Halloween Alphabet

Written by Denise Brennan-Nelson and Illustrated by Donald Wu

Text Copyright © 2009 Denise Brennan-Nelson
Illustration Copyright © 2009 Donald Wu

Sleeping Bear Press™
310 North Main Street, Suite 300
Chelsea, MI 48118
www.sleepingbearpress.com

© 2009 Sleeping Bear Press is an imprint of Gale, a part of Cengage Learning.

Printed and bound in China.

First Edition

10 9 8 7 6 5 4 3 2 1

Library of Congress Cataloging-in-Publication Data

Brennan-Nelson, Denise.
J is for jack-o-lantern : a halloween alphabet / written by Denise Brennan-Nelson ;
illustrated by Donald Wu.
p. cm.
ISBN 978-1-58536-443-5
1. Halloween—Juvenile literature. I. Wu, Donald, ill. II. Title.
GT4965.B74 2009
394.2646—dc22   2009004808

To Becca Boo. I love you.

DENISE

☾

For Robert

DONALD

In Autumn the days become shorter and the nights cooler. It is the season when most crops are harvested, deciduous trees lose their leaves, and birds and butterflies migrate to warmer climates.

The first day of autumn is known as the autumnal equinox, which occurs when the position of the sun makes the length of day and night equal for all parts of the world. In addition to the many changes, autumn brings us Halloween.

It is easy to fall into autumn's splendor. Every year Mother Nature paints the autumn landscape with her fiery show of colors. Tourists that flock to see autumn's spectacular show are called "leaf peepers."

Did you know leaves are really orange, red, yellow, and brown all year long? We can't see these colors because the green pigment chlorophyll dominates during the growing season. Toward the end of summer as the trees begin to go dormant, the chlorophyll begins to weaken and the other pigments become more visible.

A is for Autumn

A is for autumn—
blazing colors so bright.
Cider mills, pumpkins,
and Halloween night.

A
a

B b

B is for boo,
bones, and bat.
Don't forget broomstick,
brew, and black cat.

There are many symbols associated with Halloween. Images of bad omens such as black cats, bats, and broomsticks are commonly used to create the magic of the season.

It wouldn't be Halloween without bats hanging around. They have a bad reputation despite the fact they're harmless and help keep the mosquito population down.

Most bats eat fruit and insects but there is such a thing as a vampire bat. It is the only mammal that feeds on blood. It lives in Central and South America and needs about one tablespoon of blood a day to survive. It uses its sharp incisor teeth to cut holes in its victims, usually cattle, and then sucks the blood.

During the Middle Ages it was believed that witches could turn themselves into black cats. In the United States and European countries it is thought to be bad luck if a black cat crosses your path but in Japan and the United Kingdom it is thought to be good luck.

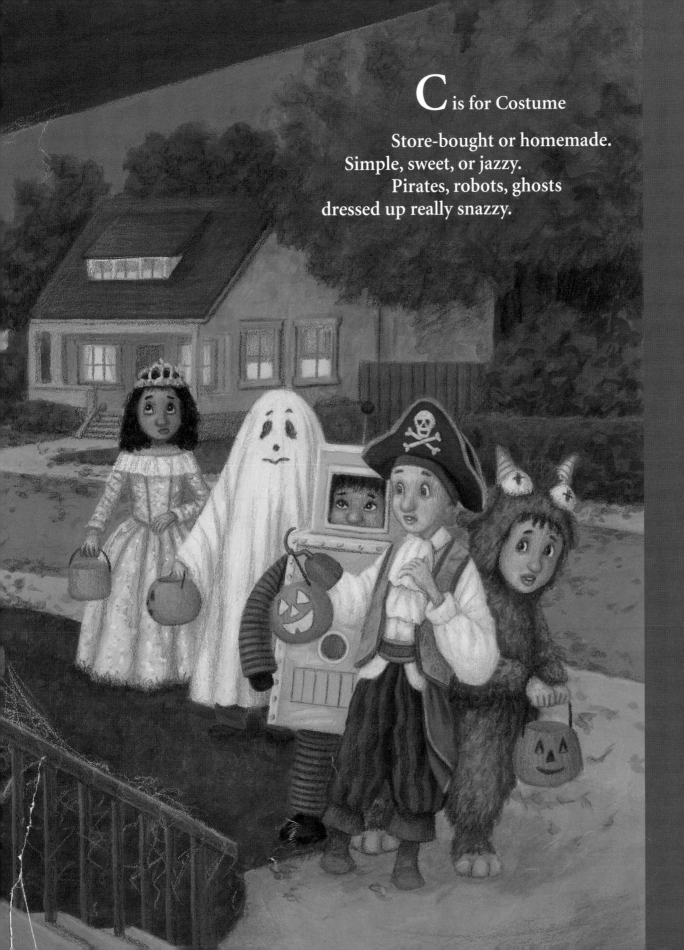

C is for Costume

Store-bought or homemade.
Simple, sweet, or jazzy.
Pirates, robots, ghosts
dressed up really snazzy.

Wearing costumes is a Halloween tradition that goes back to the Celts, a group of people who lived in Ireland, Britain, and northern France.

They held a festival called Samhain (summer's end) to celebrate the end of harvest and the beginning of their new year. Their new year started on November 1st, so they celebrated the night before, which is October 31st.

The Celts believed that the souls of the dead came back this night to roam the Earth. They began wearing masks and blackening their faces with soot during the festival to frighten the evil spirits away. They also carved turnips and gourds and lit them with glowing coals.

As time went on, people began to dress up and perform antics to get food and drink. This was called "mumming" and may be how trick-or-treating evolved.

It wasn't until the 1950s that costumes were mass-produced and sold in stores.

Cc

Halloween games are so much fun. Here's a simple yummy one:

Bobbing for Donuts Game

You'll Need:

- String
- Donuts with holes
- Somewhere to hang the donuts: tree, broomstick handle, clothesline.

How to play:

Gently tie a string onto the donut. Hang the donut by the string. Players then take turns holding their hands behind their backs while trying to bite the hanging donut. Each player gets his or her own donut.

To make it more difficult and fun, try blind-folding players first.

D is also for doorbell, disguise, delicious, delightful, dreadful, and decorations. What other Halloween words can you think of that start with the letter D?

D d

D is for Donuts on a string

Dangle donuts from a string
    and cover each player's eyes.
Now be the first to finish
    and win a kooky prize.

Ee

An eye may be small but it does a big job! Eyes are complex and efficient organs with many parts to them. Some supply tears, while others protect the eye from injury. These and other parts work together to provide us with our invaluable sense of sight. Did you know the fastest moving muscle in the human body is the one that opens and closes the eyelid?

Make this easy, edible, eyeball recipe for your next Halloween party and hear your friends go EEK!

Deviled egg eyeballs
Ingredients:
  1 dozen hardboiled eggs, peeled
  Mayonnaise
  24 green olives with pimentos
  Pinch of dry yellow mustard
  Salt to taste
  Toothpicks
  Red food coloring (paste works best)

Directions:
Cut the eggs in half lengthwise. Scoop out the yolks into a bowl. Set whites aside. Mash egg yolks with fork. Mix in mayonnaise, mustard, and salt. Stir well. Place 1 teaspoon of mixture in each half of egg whites.

Push a green olive into the center of the egg yolk mixture, making sure the red pimento is "looking" out.

Dip toothpick in red food coloring and make "red veins" in the yolk mixture. Enjoy!

E is also for eek, eerie, evil, and enticing.

E is for Eyeballs

Eyeballs floating in the punch.
A gruesome snack or maybe lunch.
Big and round and bleary red,
looking gooey, filled with dread.

Ff

F is for Frankenstein

Frankenstein is famous,
frightening, freaky, too.
Create a monster of your own
and see what he can do.

In 1818 Mary Shelley, then 19 years old, wrote a novel titled *Frankenstein.*

Frankenstein was mistakenly thought of as the monster, but Victor Frankenstein was actually the scientist who created the monster.

As the story goes, Doctor Frankenstein spent months creating a creature out of body parts. One night, while working in his laboratory, his creation came to life. But instead of being overjoyed, Victor Frankenstein was horrified at what he had done.

At first the monster was a loving creature, but as he experienced rejection because of his appearance he became violent and full of hatred.

Classic horror films such as *Frankenstein* have inspired many Halloween costumes.

The creature Frankenstein created in Shelley's book never had a name. He was referred to as "monster," "wretch," "devil," "fiend." What name would you have given him?

Gg

Ghost sightings are not nearly as rare as you might think. Many cultures in the world believe that ghosts exist, and ghost stories can be traced back as far as 2000 B.C. Some people are so intrigued by ghosts that they hunt and investigate them and call themselves ghost hunters. They have equipment and procedures they use to record ghost sightings and believe that ghost activity is increased during the full and new phases of the moon.

The use of ghosts in Halloween celebrations is thought to have originated with the Druids, a class of citizens of the Celtic society. They believed that ghosts, spirits, fairies, witches, and elves came out on Halloween to harm people.

There are numerous stories about ghosts in the White House. Imagine sleeping in the White House and having the ghost of Abe Lincoln show up at your bedside.

Do you believe in ghosts?

Some ghastly jokes for you!
Q: *What's a ghouls favorite breakfast food?*
Q: *What do little ghosts drink?*
Q: *What do ghosts serve for dessert?*
(You'll have to ask a ghost for the answers. Or look in the back of the book.)

G is for Ghosts

Ghosts and ghouls and goblins
play gruesome, gooey, gags.
Throw parties in the graveyard
with ghastly, giggly hags.

H is for Haunted House

A haunted house; you better beware.
Only enter if you dare.
Monsters lurking, looking mean—
just can't wait to make you scream!

Haunted houses are usually avoided except around Halloween! Creeping through a haunted house can be a harrowing experience. Your hair stands on end, a tingle runs down your spine, and you may hear screams and cries for help! But it's all for Halloween fun!

What makes a house haunted? Unexplained things happen; shadows dance, doors open by themselves, lights flicker on and off. In haunted houses there is a way out for those whose "quaking knees" won't let them finish the tour. It's called "the chicken door."

Most haunted houses are created by people who like a thrill. If you like to be scared, a visit to a haunted house will definitely do the "trick."

H is also for Halloween. Halloween dates back over 3,000 years ago to a Celtic celebration. The Celts celebrated their New Year's Day on November 1st. They called it "All Hallows Day." October 31st became "All Hallows Eve" and in time was shortened to "Halloween."

H h

I i

What would Halloween be without an ooey-gooey Halloween game to play? For this fun Halloween game you will need:

- Hot dog chunks or end of a pickle: *nose*
- Whole cooked, chilled cauliflower: *brain*
- Peeled grapes or black olives: *eyeballs*
- Cooked spaghetti noodles: *intestines*
- Dried apricots: *ears*
- Slab of gelatin: *liver*
- Nut shells: *toenails*
- Pieces of chalk: *teeth*
- Wet fur or yarn: *hair*
- Latex glove, filled with warm water, tied and frozen: *hand*
- Small amount of ketchup thinned with warm water: *blood*

Place the body parts in re-sealable plastic bags, then put each "body part" in separate paper bags so game players can't see them. Dim the lights and sit in a circle. Pass the bags around one at a time and have everyone reach into each bag without looking and guess the "body part." (Have paper towels handy.) Give a prize to the one with the most correct answers.

I is for Icky

An "icky" Halloween game to play
if you're not faint of heart
requires you to feel and match
the food with the body part.

J j

J is for Jack-o'-lantern

A crooked grin or a carrot nose,
how 'bout a smiling face?
J is for your jack-o'-lantern,
a pumpkin with a face.

Glowing jack-o'-lanterns capture the spirit and magic of Halloween. A jack-o'-lantern is a carved pumpkin and one of the most recognizable decorations of Halloween. Carving turnips and beets is a very old Halloween custom that dates back to Ireland and the Celts. They would carve ugly faces into the turnips and beets to scare away any bad spirits. Pumpkins then became the popular choice.

The term jack-o'-lantern first appeared in print in 1750. At that time it referred to a night watchman or a man carrying a lantern.

According to *The Guinness Book of World Records*, the record for the most lit jack-o'-lanterns on display is 30,128 in Boston, Massachusetts in October 2006.

K k

K is for King-size

Some neighbors give out apples,
licorice, gum, a toy.
But when I see that king-size bar,
I can't help but jump for joy!

More candy is bought for Halloween than any other holiday, but sweet treats have been enjoyed by people for thousands of years. Honey straight from beehives is thought to be the first. Fruits and nuts were then added to the honey, paving the way for what would become the first candy bar. It wasn't until the 1890s that the first milk chocolate bar was made.

Has your favorite candy ever suddenly disappeared from your treat bag? According to a poll by the National Confectioner's Association, ninety percent of parents admitted to sneaking candy from their kids' bags.

The world's largest lollipop weighed over 4,000 pounds. What flavor do you think it was?

L is for Light

Pass by the house
that has no light.
It's their way of saying,
"No candy tonight!"

Not everyone enjoys Halloween. Some people avoid trick-or-treaters by pretending they're not home. They pull their shades, turn off all their lights, and keep their doors shut. So if you come upon a dark house, keep going!

On the other hand, sometimes people can't be home on Halloween and set a bowl of candy on their porches for trick-or-treaters. A trusting, generous gesture, don't you agree?

Ll

M is for Maze

A corn maze is a puzzle
where you can stroll about.
Have fun getting lost,
then find your way back out.

Six-foot-high cornstalks border narrow passages; twists and turns bewilder and confuse you. Everything looks the same and makes getting lost easy as you search and scramble for the exit to the corn maze.

A corn maze, or labyrinth is a puzzle cut into a cornfield. Some have simple pathways and are fun and easy to "solve," while others are elaborate designs that test your navigational skills.

Not all mazes are made from cornfields. Hedges, trees, and stone walls have been used to design mazes.

Mazes have been traced back as far as 2400 B.C. Ancient mazes were used as a form of artwork and entertainment in gardens. Mazes could be found in the formal gardens of castles and palaces throughout Europe for the amusement of kings.

You can find corn mazes in every state and they are quickly becoming a way for farmers to earn extra income. The largest corn maze in the world is located in Dixon, California, and is 40 acres in area.

M
m

N n

The days leading up to Halloween are fun and festive but it isn't until Halloween night that the real fun begins! Jack-o'-lanterns illuminate porches, and neighborhoods across the country are filled with trick-or-treaters in mischievous costumes.

If you think Halloween night is magical where you live, imagine trick-or-treating in one of the following places:

- Transylvania County, North Carolina
- Cape Fear, North Carolina
- Tombstone, Arizona
- Gnaw Bone, Indiana
- Frankenstein, Missouri
- Bat Cave, North Carolina
- Pumpkin Center, Oklahoma

N is for Nighttime

Nighttime brings spooky sounds.
Shadows darting all around.
Coyotes sing an eerie tune
as witches fly around the moon.

When you think of a pumpkin, the color orange comes to mind. But not all pumpkins are orange. There are white, gray, red, and even blue pumpkins!

Orange symbolizes fall's harvest and is a traditional Halloween color.

The full moon closest to the autumnal equinox is called the harvest moon. This usually occurs in September but about once every four years it occurs in October.

The harvest moon appears bigger and brighter than other full moons and most likely got its name because it helped farmers harvest their crops. It is also known as wine moon, singing moon, and elk call moon.

There are many rituals and festivals to celebrate the harvest moon. And in some cultures, if your birthday falls on or near a harvest moon, you are responsible for providing a feast for your community.

O is for Orange

The color of pumpkins
        and the harvest moon.
Fall is orange
        but *leaves* too soon.

P is for Pumpkin Patch

Pick a pumpkin from a patch.
No two pumpkins are a match.
Cut the vine, but if they're fat
don't pick them up or they'll go splat!

Pp

The pumpkin originated in Mexico about 9000 years ago. "Pumpkin" comes from the Greek word for "large melon," which is "pepon."

Native Americans used pumpkins in a variety of ways, from eating them to drying strips of pumpkins to make into mats.

Pumpkins are a fruit that belongs to the cucurbitacae family, which includes cucumbers, melon, and squash. Pumpkins grow on a green bushy vine along the ground. Male and female blossoms appear and open for a day. The pollen from the male blossom is transferred to the female flowers by bees, and then the pollinated blossoms develop into pumpkins.

Pumpkin plants are hearty and strong and a pumpkin vine can grow as much as six inches a day! They need a sunny spot and a lot of water to grow and thrive. By late August the green pumpkins will begin to change colors. About four months after planting, they're ready to be harvested.

Antarctica is the only continent where pumpkins cannot grow.

Q q

Q is for Quivering and Quaking

Quivering lips
and quaking knees.
Don't wake the ghosts!
Quiet, please!

Why do some people love to be scared? It may have to do with the physical changes that occur in our bodies and how these changes heighten and sharpen our senses when we're frightened.

Our heart pumps faster and harder which sends more blood into our muscles. It is our body's way of getting prepared for quick action but it can make us quiver or tremble with energy. The extra blood pumping through our veins can also generate more heat which can cause our bodies to sweat.

Other physical changes can occur in our bodies when we are afraid; our mouths go dry, our chest and throat tighten, goose bumps may appear on our skin, and our pupils dilate.

R is for Rattling bones

Skeletons party in abandoned homes.
R is for their rattling bones.
They shake and boogie across the floor.
Dance until their bones are sore!

Skeletons are a favorite Halloween symbol. A full body skeleton hanging on the porch or a bag of bones scattered about are enough to scare the heebie-jeebies out of anyone! Why is that? They're just bones!

A newborn baby has approximately 270 bones, while an average adult human has 206 bones. This network of bones is called our skeleton. It protects our internal organs, supports the body's shape and allows our muscles to move our limbs. Bones continue to form years after birth and stop sometime between the ages of 13 and 19. How many can you name?

The longest and heaviest bone is the femur and the shortest is the stapes. Do you know where they are located? (The femur is located in the thigh and the stapes is in the middle ear.)

Mexico has a holiday similar to Halloween called "Day of the Dead." It is a celebration to honor loved ones that have passed away. It is a festive and colorful holiday and the skeleton plays a key role in the festival.

Rr

S is for Scarecrow

Scarecrows hang around all day;
wear old clothes filled with hay.
They work to chase the crows away
but when do scarecrows get to play?

For hundreds of years farmers have used scarecrows in their gardens and fields to keep crows and other unwanted birds from eating the crops they grow. Traditionally they were made from old clothes stuffed with straw or hay and secured to two large sticks. The birds were tricked into thinking it was a real farmer and were frightened away.

Now, people use scarecrows as part of their festive fall decoration. Propped up on bales of hay smiling or standing on their heads, they are a fun and sometimes scary Halloween prop.

In Japanese mythology, a scarecrow appears as a supreme being who cannot walk, but knows everything of the world.

Use your imagination and create your own scarecrow! They can be humorous, gruesome, or, glamorous, too!

S s

T t

There are different theories about how trick-or-treating began. One of them involves the Celtic festival Samhain, (sow-en) which was held to celebrate the end of summer. During this time some believe that villagers would dress up in costumes to scare away evil spirits. Others think they dressed up to make the spirits feel more comfortable. In addition, to keep the spirits happy the Celtic people left food and drink outside their houses on Halloween. If any hungry spirits came by, they could take the food and leave the Celtics in peace.

Another theory dates back to the early celebration of All Soul's Day in Britain. The poor would go from village to village begging for food. They received treats called "soulcakes" (square pieces of bread with currants in them). In exchange, the beggars would say a prayer for the dead. This was called "going-a-souling." If the beggars didn't receive "treats," they would threaten to play a "trick" on the homeowner or his property.

Trick-or-treating is also known as guising in parts of England. In Scotland, the children sing a song or tell a joke or funny poem in order to get a treat. Some children may even do magic tricks in order to get candy.

T is also for thank you, two of the sweetest words.

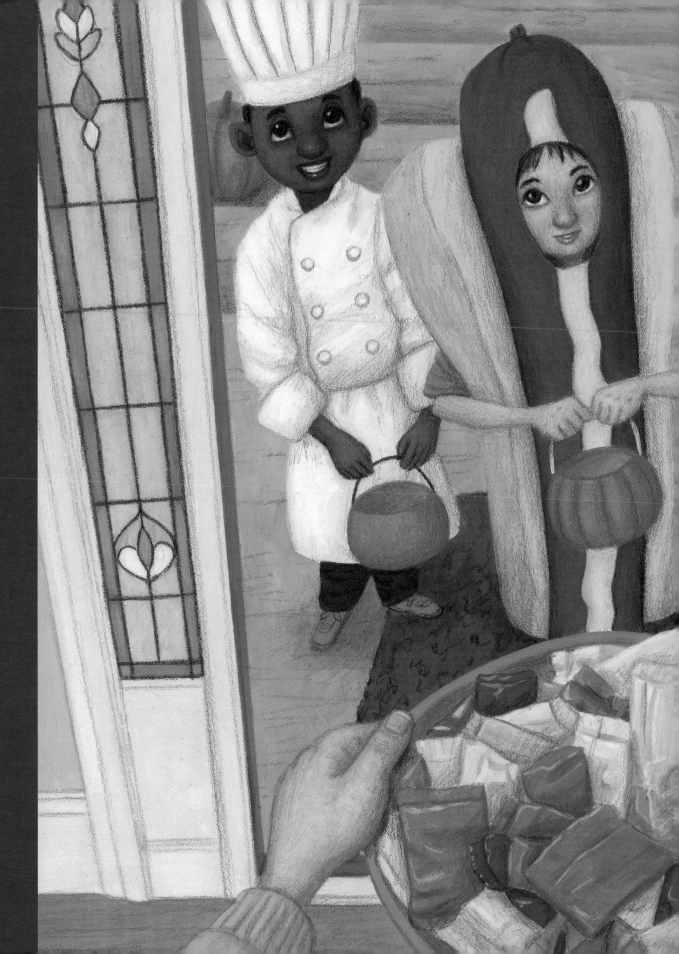

T is for Trick-or-treat

Three simple words you must repeat
    if you desire something sweet.
The magic words are:
        "Trick-or-Treat!"

U is for Unusual

U is for unusual—
my Halloween disguise.
So unique and utterly cool,
my costume wins first prize!

What's the most unusual costume you've ever seen? A slice of pizza? How about a banana, or a skunk?

There are many Halloween stores with costumes to choose from. Or, with a little imagination you can come up with an unusual costume that will make others ask, "Now how did they think of that?" Movies, music, books, food, political figures...even household objects are great places to look when you're thinking about your Halloween costume.

It takes creativity and a good sense of humor to come up with a unique and unusual costume. Aim to be different and stand out from everyone else!

Here are a few unusual costume ideas to get you thinking:

- *twins*
- *crayons*
- *Rubik's cube*
- *cotton candy*
- *stoplight*
- *Christmas tree*

- *couch potato*
- *hot air balloon*
- *bubble bath*
- *sushi*
- *s'more*
- *deviled egg*

U u

V is for Vampire

He came to life by sucking blood.
A vampire with fame—
he lived in Transylvania,
Count Dracula was his name.

Vampires are mythical creatures and go back thousands of years. In folklore, vampires do not die. Their bodies rise from their graves at night and must return at dawn. They exist by feeding on the blood of the living.

The most famous vampire, Count Dracula, was created by the Irish writer Bram Stoker in 1897.

The story is loosely based on Prince Vlad from Transylvania, Romania, whose nickname was Dracula. He was born in 1431 into a noble family. His father's name was Dracula which means dragon or devil, making Vlad "son of the dragon." Historians believe this was the beginning of the legend that Dracula was a vampire.

Vampire lore describes them as compulsive counters, so throwing poppy seeds on the ground in cemeteries will keep vampires busy counting until they must return to their coffin at dawn.

Q: Why did the vampire go to the orthodontist?
A: *To improve his bite*

Q: Why did the vampire need mouthwash?
A: *She had bat breath.*

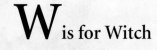

W is for Witch

      Witches are green, scary, and mean.
Brooms keep them in motion.
      They gather 'round their big black pots
to stir their magic potion.

What image comes to mind when you hear the word "witch?" An ugly, old woman riding on a broom with her black cat, casting evil spells?

That wasn't always the case. The word "witch" comes from the Old Saxon word "wica," meaning "wise one." The earliest witches were dealers in charms and medicinal herbs and tellers of fortunes.

The idea of a witch goes back to Greek and Roman gods and goddesses who were thought to be magical. At one time being a witch was considered a sign of good fortune.

However, the notions of witchcraft and good fortune changed and witches were seen as evil. In the American colonies, anyone thought to be a witch or practicing witchcraft would be tried in a court of law and if convicted, would be put to death.

The Salem Witch Trials (Salem, Massachusetts) in 1692 are the most famous witch trials and resulted in the largest witch hunt in American history. One hundred and fifty people were arrested and nineteen of them were found guilty and put to death.

What can be more fun than coming home and dumping your Halloween bag out on the living room floor; sorting, counting, trading ...eating! But before you sink your teeth into a candy bar, let a grown-up check it out.

Candy tampering is rare but it has happened. It is best to trick or treat only in areas you are familiar with. Make sure the candy is unopened and remove any items that may cause an allergic reaction.

Some towns encourage parents to bring their Halloween candy to the local hospital or fire station to be x-rayed to make sure that it's safe.

X
x

X is for eXamination

What's inside your candy?
Parents like to know
if your treats are safe.
A simple eXam will show.

Yy

Y is for Yard

Yards reflect this festive time
with surprises and delights.
Pumpkins, coffins, scarecrows,
and don't forget the lights!

Halloween is the second most popular holiday for decorating in the United States. Setting the mood for Halloween can be quick, easy, and wickedly fun!

People begin decorating their houses and yards for Halloween as summer wanes and the leaves begin to change. The decorating possibilities are endless! Find inspiration simply by taking a drive and checking out yards in nearby neighborhoods or browsing around a Halloween store.

Some yards have elaborate displays with lighting effects that cast creepy shadows, fog machines that make you wonder what's lurking around, and scary sculpted jack-o'-lanterns. Others prefer a more traditional theme using scarecrows, bales of hay, and cornstalks.

Whether you turn your yard into a ghastly graveyard or a festive and friendly place, decorating your yard for Halloween is sure to delight you and the visitors that pass by your house.

Zz

Halloween is a unique holiday that is enthusiastically celebrated around the world. It began as a holiday for children but it has grown popular with adults, making Halloween a time for everyone!

It's not solely historical or patriotic, as is the Fourth of July and Thanksgiving. And unlike Christmas, Hanukkah, Passover, or Easter it is not part of one particular religion. Instead, Halloween reflects a variety of origins.

Halloween is more than the candy and the decorations. It's steeped in history and traditions that will continue to be passed on through the years.

Z is for Zany

Halloween is zany fun—
a holiday for everyone!
Young and old have a reason
to enjoy this lively season.

Halloween Tricks and Treats

Making the most of your jack-o'-lantern:
Once a pumpkin is carved it doesn't last very long, especially in warm temperatures. Keeping them cool and out of the sun will help them last longer.

A pumpkin begins to shrivel up as it loses moisture. Soaking them overnight in water helps to restore the moisture. Another trick is to coat them with petroleum jelly, including the inside, as soon as you have carved them.

It's best not to carry your pumpkin by its stem. If the stem does break off, try using toothpicks to put it back in place.

Bobbing for apples is one of the oldest Halloween games. Some think it started at a Roman festival that honored Pamona, the goddess of fruit trees.

To the Celts, bobbing for apples would determine the next one to get married. Today it is a simple and fun Halloween game.

Halloween symbols
Halloween has become a popular holiday but its origin is complex. This complexity is evident in its recognizable set of symbols.

These symbols can be broken down into three categories:

Symbols of death: *ghosts, skeletons, graveyards, haunted houses*
Symbols of evil and misfortune: *witches, goblins, black cats*
Symbols of harvest: *pumpkins, scarecrows, cornstalks, candy corn*

Halloween colors and what they symbolize:
Black: *night, witches, bats, vampires, black cats, death*
Orange: *pumpkins, autumn*
Purple: *the supernatural, mysticism, night*
Green: *goblins, monsters*
Red: *blood, evil*

Pumpkin Tidbits
- Pumpkins contain potassium and Vitamin A.
- Pumpkin flowers are edible.
- Pumpkins were once recommended for removing freckles and curing snake bites.

The record for the largest pumpkin came from Rhode Island and was a 1,689 pound pumpkin, weighed on September 29, 2007.

The Guinness Book of World Records states that the world's biggest pumpkin pie ever made is 2,020 pounds! The New Bremen Giant Pumpkin Growers in New Bremen, Ohio prepared and baked this giant pie.

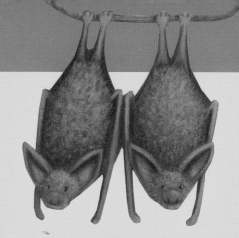

Ghosts, ghouls, and goblins

Ghost: *the soul of a dead person believed to be an inhabitant of the unseen world or to appear to the living in bodily likeness*

Ghoul: *a legendary evil being that robs graves and feeds on corpses*

Goblin: *an ugly or grotesque spirit that is usually mischievous and sometimes evil and malicious*

Ghostly Riddles

Q: What's a ghoul's favorite breakfast food?
　　A: *Rice creepies*

Q: What do little ghosts drink?
　　A: *Evaporated milk*

Q: What do ghosts serve for dessert?
　　A: *I scream*

Hot Apple Cider
Ingredients:
- 1 quart apple cider
- ½ cup brown sugar
- ½ tablespoon whole cloves
- 1 small cinnamon stick
- ⅛ teaspoon salt

Mix together and simmer 20 to 30 minutes.
(Your house will smell like autumn and apple pies. Yum.)

A Witch's Brew just for you:
Ingredients:
- 12 oz orange juice concentrate, frozen
- 12 oz white grape juice
- 2 liter bottle 7-Up
- 1 pt sherbet, lemon or lime
- Green food coloring

Mix all together and add several drops of green food coloring. Cheers!

Denise Brennan-Nelson

One of author Denise Brennan-Nelson's favorite Halloween memories is of her daughters, Rebecca and Rachel, wearing skunk costumes, homemade by Denise and her mother. Appropriate costumes, as the girls are "mommy's little stinkers."

Denise lives in Howell, Michigan with her daughters and husband Bob, who likes to scare the heebie-jeebies out of her, and not just on Halloween. Howell is home to the Opera House, built in 1881 and is believed by many to be haunted.

Denise is also the author of several other books from Sleeping Bear Press including *Willow*; *Buzzy the bumblebee*; *My Teacher Likes to Say*; *Penny: The Forgotten Coin*; *Grady the Goose*; and *Someday is Not a Day of the Week*.

Donald Wu

Donald Wu grew up in the San Francisco Bay area after moving there as a child from Hong Kong. Years of drawing doodles in school, along with a love of comic books, led him to study illustration at the California College of the Arts. His current focus is in children's book illustration, but he also has experience with portraiture and editorial artwork. Donald continues to reside and draw his "doodles" in the San Francisco Bay area.